A SUPERCHAMP BOOK

The WALLOPING STICK WAR

GWEN GRANT

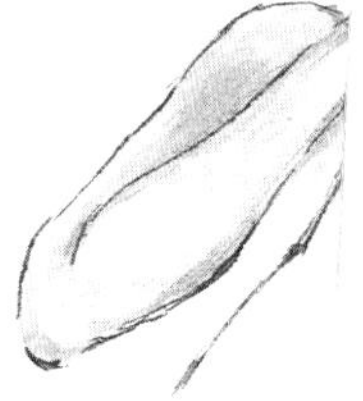

Illustrated by
KATE ALDOUS

HEINEMANN · LONDON

For my grandson, Andrew

William Heinemann Ltd
Michelin House, 81 Fulham Road,
London SW3 6RB

LONDON MELBOURNE AUCKLAND

First published 1989

ISBN 0 434 93055 5
Printed in Hong Kong by
Mandarin Offset

A school pack of SUPERCHAMPS 1–6
is available from
Heinemann Educational Books
ISBN 0 434 00090 X

Chapter One

It was a Saturday morning when Kenneth Grey found his Grandad in the living room of their flat. He was so surprised to see him, he stopped dead.

'Where did you come from?' he asked, beaming. 'Gosh, I'm glad to see you, Grandad.'

His Grandad laughed.

'And I'm glad to see you. I seem to have been travelling for ever. Why, I set off from the North two days ago, walking, hitching lifts when I could. Still, not bad going for an old man, eh? Just two days.'

Kenneth wished that he could go North with his Grandad, walking the roads, hitching lifts.

'I'm about too old and you're not old enough,' his Grandad grinned when he asked him. 'The minute you are, though, we'll be gone, you and I. But there's nothing to stop us going walking this weekend, is there?'

Kenneth felt a leap of joy.

'This weekend?' he questioned. 'You mean, today?'

'I should think today and tomorrow,' his Grandad told him. 'Why not? Your Mum says we can stop out all night tonight.'

'As long as you look after each other,' his mother put in, smiling.

'Well, I'm ready to go now,' Kenneth said quickly, in case anyone changed their mind. 'This very minute!' And turning, he dashed into his bedroom and scrambled pell-mell into jumper and jeans.

'Let your Grandad have a cup of tea first,' his mother said, when he hopped back into the living room, tugging his shoes on as he went. 'Go on, pour us all a cup. I think we could do with it.'

Kenneth poured the tea, his hand shaking with excitement. A whole weekend with his Grandad. He could hardly wait.

He jumped from one foot to the other whilst his Grandad drank his tea and ate his way through a great pile of bacon and eggs, sausage and tomatoes.

After a while, he sat down and leant against the old man's knee. The last time his Grandad had stayed with them, he had smelt of wood smoke and dry grassy fields.

Kenneth took a deep breath. It was still there, under the bacon and eggs, it was still the same. An earthy woody smell that reminded him of chestnutting and bonfire night.

At long last, his Grandad put his cup down and looked at Kenneth.

'Well, I'm ready if you are.'

'Have you had a wash?' his mother asked, and Kenneth tore through to the bathroom, sprinkled his face with water, cleaned his teeth in three seconds flat and was back out again, standing by the door. 'Come on, Grandad. Let's go.'

'Anorak,' Mrs Grey said firmly. 'It could turn cold – or rain – and I don't want you coming back ill.'

Kenneth sighed loudly, but one glance at his mother's face told him he had to go back and get his anorak.

When he had the coat under his arm, his mother smiled at them both.

'Have a good time and do as Grandad tells you, Kenneth.'

'Yes, yes,' Kenneth said impatiently and tugged at the old man's hand.

Mrs Grey opened the front door for them and they stepped into the dusty concrete corridor. It always looked dirty

3·4·5·6

and dark. The door closed firmly behind them and Grandad looked at the concrete, at the wire meshed windows and shook his head. He was glad Kenneth was going away for the weekend.

'A bit of fresh air will do you good,' he said.

'I'll get the lift up,' Kenneth offered and punched the button that would bring the lift.

They could hear it, whining and wailing its way through the building. Finally, it clanked and shuddered to a halt in front of them and the doors opened.

The moment he looked into the lift, Kenneth's heart sank. He wished yet again that they lived on the ground floor and didn't have to take the lift at all because there, crammed into the small square space, was Mincer Muggs and his gang. There seemed a million of them, sitting on each other's shoulders, leaning against the sides of the lift, squatting on the floor. There didn't look room enough for a fly.

Grandad Rogers didn't seem to see them. He just stepped into the lift and almost trod on several of Mincer's gang.

Yelping and shouting, they bellowed, 'Watch out, old man, can't you? Watch what you're doing!' But Grandad Rogers stood in the middle of them all as if no-one were there but him and Kenneth.

Kenneth stood at the old man's side, Mincer's ugly face leaning over his shoulder.

'Get off, Mincer,' Kenneth snapped and pushed at the boy's face with his open hand.

'I'll tear your head off yer neck,' Mincer snarled and then Grandad started to tell Kenneth about his walking stick.

'See this?' he said, and even though he was only talking to Kenneth, everybody in the lift nodded their heads. 'This is a walnut walloping stick.' He bounced it on the floor and it made a sharp cracking sound. 'A walloping stick, that's what this is. When you've been walloped by walnut, take it from me, you stay walloped.'

The Muggs gang looked at the stick, then at the old man with his sharp face and keen eyes, and hurriedly edged away from him. Mincer didn't move. He was too busy tormenting Kenneth, poking him in the back, sticking his tongue out, pinching, jabbing, until Kenneth would have lashed out at him if his Grandad hadn't been there.

Mincer sniffed.

'Yerk,' he said, then sniffed again, a horrible, wet, noisy sniff.

''Ere,' he said suddenly. 'Your Grandad stinks.'

He prodded Kenneth sharply in the back.

1 • 2 • 3 • 4 • 5 • 6

'Didja hear me?' he demanded. 'I said your potty old Grandad stinks.'

This was too much and Kenneth whirled round, fists doubled up.

'You shut up!' he said fiercely. 'I'll flatten you, Mincer, if you say that again. My Grandad doesn't stink. It's you that stinks, so just shut up.'

'And you just make me,' Mincer jeered, looming over Kenneth. 'Go on, you just make me shut up.'

'Get 'im, Mince!' his pals cried. 'Smash 'im to a pulp. Tear 'is head orf. Stamp on his fingers and make raspberry jam!' And they laughed. Great sneering howls of laughter.

All Kenneth's blood seemed to be beating in his head. His legs went weak and shaky. He thought for a minute he was going to fall down and had to press his lips together hard and ball his fists up so tightly, he could feel the edges of his finger nails cutting into the skin.

'I'll make you shut up, all right,' he said and hoped his voice didn't shake.

For a moment, it seemed there would be a terrible fight in the lift. The Muggs gang grew quiet and pulled away, watching with silent, mean eyes.

But with a bump, the lift landed on the ground floor and Grandad Rogers whistled cheerfully as the doors opened. He could see daylight. He could smell fresh air.

He banged the walloping stick on the ground and it leapt in the air, almost seeming to rap knuckles and crack shins of its own accord. He bounced it again and the lift was filled with shrieks as the walloping stick somehow managed to rattle against everyone.

''Ere! Get off. Get out!' Mincer cried

as the walnut stick gave him a vicious rap on the knee.

Grandad Rogers strode jauntily out of the lift, dragging Kenneth behind him.

'What did I tell you?' he asked. 'When you've been walloped with a

walloping stick, you stay walloped.'
And without even a backward glance, he was marching to the door.

Mincer shot out of the lift.

'Yah! Yahhhhh!' he yelled. 'You're scared, Kenneth Grey. You're scared, that's what you are. Hiding behind your Grandad, that's what you're doing. Come back here and put your fists up.'

Kenneth struggled, trying to get free of Grandad's hand, trying to get back to Mincer – but his Grandad didn't seem to notice he was struggling and just marched on, cracking his walnut stick against the floor with every step.

'You and your Grandad,' Mincer roared nastily. 'He ain't nothing but a gypsy. That's what he is. Him and his walnut stick. They stink, both of them. He ain't nothing but a mucky old gyppo.'

Kenneth was so mad by now he didn't feel scared at all.

'Let go of my arm, Grandad,' he yelled. 'I'm going to pulverise that Muggs. I'm going to flatten him. I'm going to . . . to . . . just let me go. Let me go!' But his Grandad didn't answer and he didn't slow down and he didn't let go of Kenneth's arm.

After a while, when there didn't seem much point in struggling and shouting, Kenneth fell silent. His Grandad let go of him, grinned, and trying to forget Mincer Muggs, they marched on together, side by side.

Chapter Two

THE FLATS GRANDAD and Kenneth were walking through were like great dark canyons. You had to lift your head up and tip it back to see the top of them. The sun had gone in, making the streets darker than ever.

When they got to a small row of shops, Grandad said, 'I'm going to get us some milk and rolls, Kenneth. You wait here a minute. I shan't be long.'

Kenneth nodded and leant against the shop windows. His Grandad was almost into the shop when he came back out again.

'Take the walloping stick,' he said, thoughtfully. 'Just in case.'

Kenneth took the shiny stick into his

hand. The fox head top was smooth where his Grandad's hand polished it, the warm skin rubbing against the dark wood.

He wandered to the end of the shops and just as he got to the corner, a bottle came flying out of the sky and crashed at his feet.

Kenneth whirled round. Mincer and his gang were behind him.

'Where's the old man?' Mincer asked. 'We've come for you both. To get our own back, see!'

Some of the boys edged round so that Kenneth soon saw he was surrounded.

'Keep away,' he said as calmly as he could. 'Keep away from me.'

Mincer laughed, his hard voice sounding like the hard voice of a crow.

'Keep away?' he taunted. 'Keep away? Now, 'oos going to keep us away?'

'I am,' Kenneth said slowly and lifted the walloping stick.

'That's not going to save you,' Mincer sneered. Then, looking at his gang, he shouted, 'Go on, then. What're you waiting for?' And the gang rushed at Kenneth, punching and shoving in their eagerness to get at him.

Kenneth backed into the wall. He lifted the walnut stick and swung it round him. One by one the boys in the gang fell back.

'I told you. I warned you,' Kenneth shouted.

Mincer moved back a little, then forward. Kenneth jabbed at him with the walking stick. Then, Grandad Rogers came out of the shop.

'Get 'im!' Mincer shouted. 'Get the old man!' And the Muggs gang began to hurl things at Grandad Rogers.

Bottles, stones, halves of bricks. The objects rained down on Grandad and made him duck and hurry back to shelter.

Kenneth darted forward and swung the stick at the gang. They were wise to him now, they laughed and jumped out of the way but he was so fast on his feet, he caught some of them with the walloping stick, making them shout.

Mincer Muggs called his gang off and they ran, ran up the steep hill, back into the dark streets of the flats.

Kenneth ran after them. He could

hear his Grandad shouting to him to stop.

'Don't go after them. It's a trick. Don't go alone. Come back, Kenneth! Stay in the open.' But Kenneth was so angry he ran and ran after the Muggs gang.

He tore up the steep hill, hearing only the jeers and taunts of Mincer. He whirled round the corner and . . . stopped. There was no-one there. The gang had all vanished. The street was empty, dark and quite silent.

Kenneth looked round. There was nothing to see. He felt nervous. He waited, but nothing happened. He breathed a huge sigh of relief. They had gone. He and the walloping stick had seen them off. At last, he and Grandad could get on with their walk.

He turned to go back down the hill

and a dustbin at the side of the road suddenly erupted into life. Mincer leapt out of it, and stood in front of him. Kenneth tried to dodge but other boys dropped from windowsills, drifted out from behind half closed doors, clambered out of old boxes left for the dustbin men and grabbed hold of him.

'Let go of me!' Kenneth shouted, but Mincer just grinned.

'Oh yes, we'll let go of you all right.' Reaching forward, he tugged the walloping stick out of Kenneth's hand. 'Fond of this, aren't you?' he jeered. 'Well, so you should be because I'm going to give *you* a taste of this 'ere walloping stick.'

Kenneth shut his eyes and tensed his body, ready for the blows he felt sure were coming.

'All right,' Mincer growled. 'Stick 'im in.'

Kenneth was heaved into the air, the gang of lads yelling with laughter as they pulled forward the dustbin Mincer Muggs had hidden in.

'Push him in and shove him down,' Mincer said sourly, his face cold and set.

The Muggs gang shoved Kenneth into the bin and crushed him down. He could hardly breathe. It smelt awful. His knees were jammed under his nose. His elbows were crushed round his chest.

'That smells like your Grandad,' Mincer shouted down at him then rattled the stick along the side of the bin. The noise was deafening.

Kenneth clamped his hands over his ears.

'Don't you like it there?' Mincer asked, gloating over the trapped boy. 'Well, well, what a shame. He don't like it in there,' he told his gang and they kicked the bin,

smacking at Kenneth's head and pulling his hair.

'You're going for a ride, you are,' Mincer said at last and the heavy rubber lid was slammed on top of Kenneth.

It felt terrible in the bin. With a fearful crash, Mincer knocked it on its side and Kenneth started to feel sick as it began to rumble over and over. He realised with a shock of horror that the Muggs gang were going to send him jolting and smashing down the steep hill.

He tried to brace himself against the metal sides as, with a last thunderous roll of the walloping stick, the bin was pushed out on its own.

Kenneth thought he would never get out alive. The metal container bounced and banged its way down the hard pavement and when it finally hit against a lamp post, shooting him out, his head was ringing with noise and every bone in his body ached.

His Grandad hurried up and helped the boy to his feet.

'I can't stand,' Kenneth muttered, staggering. 'I feel so dizzy.'

Grandad Rogers helped him to the side of the road. 'Sit down a minute and rest,' he said. 'You just sit quiet and get your breath back.'

Kenneth rested. At the top of the hill, Mincer Muggs and his gang appeared.

'Get out!' they shouted. 'Go on, get out and stay out because if you don't, there's plenty more where that came from.'

Grandad Rogers looked at the boys for a long time and then he said slowly, 'Someone's going to have to teach them a lesson. Bullies always have to be taught a lesson sooner or later.'

Kenneth agreed, but sitting by the side of the road, covered in bruises with his head ringing and whirling round, he wasn't sure how the lesson was going to be taught, nor who was going to teach it.

Chapter Three

IT WAS ONLY when Kenneth and Grandad had started their walk again that Kenneth remembered he had lost the walloping stick.

'I'm sorry, Grandad,' he said. 'But Mincer grabbed it off me. I was stupid to fall into his trap, going up there on my own. Stupid,' he repeated bitterly.

His Grandad glanced at him.

'Don't let it worry you. Experience is a great teacher. It's like the walloping stick. Once you've been clouted, you never forget it.'

Kenneth nodded glumly. He knew he wouldn't forget the events of that day.

The two of them walked on, a steady fresh wind whistling round their ears, filling Kenneth's mouth with sweetness and blowing away his angry words.

He soon felt a lot better.

'I'll be glad when I can get a wash,' he said, itching and scratching. 'That bin was filthy. I feel as if things are crawling all over me.'

'We can stop by the next river,' his Grandad offered but the next river was a long time coming and Kenneth grew more and more uncomfortable.

They walked for miles, looking for a good spot to camp. The flats were left far behind. The wind dropped and the sun shone and at last, they saw the welcome sight of free running water. Kenneth didn't stop to think. He tore across to the river, pulling his clothes off as he ran. He couldn't wait to feel the cool fresh water on his skin and to rub away, once and for all, the awful memory of the dustbin. When he thought of it, he could feel his face colouring.

He'd get his own back on that Mincer Muggs, he determined. Just wait and see.

Flinging his shoes behind him, he plunged into the cold water and splashed and swam until he started to feel clean again. Until the hateful itching had stopped.

His Grandad washed slowly and carefully.

Kenneth scooped up the water, flinging it in the air. It splashed down on him in small icy fingers and he realised he was getting cold.

Slowly, his Grandad unpacked the rucksack and took out a towel. Kenneth rubbed himself dry until he felt as if he were glowing.

Grandad Rogers found a clump of willows by the waterside. He cut and stripped one of the springy wands.

'Here, clean your teeth with that,' he said and handed the boy the fleshy piece of wood.

Cautiously, Kenneth started to clean his teeth. The thin pliable wood zipped up and down, in and out of his teeth. It wasn't at all like a toothbrush.

'Finish off with a couple of mint leaves and you'll feel a new man,' his Grandad said.

They searched for the wild mint, crushing a leaf here and a leaf there, until one leaf sent out its sharp minty scent.

Carefully, Kenneth pulled off three leaves each.

He and his Grandad chewed and spat. Spat and chewed.

'Better not swallow it,' Grandad advised.

Sighing with happiness, Kenneth sat down and unpacked the milk and rolls his Grandad had bought. They sat in the sunshine eating their meal.

'I could stop here for ever. I wish we didn't have to live in the flats,' he said, looking round him at the trees and the fields and the bright river.

'Do you think that lad and his gang will come out here?' his Grandad asked and Kenneth shook his head.

'No, I don't think so. They wouldn't know what to do out of the town. They'd be lost with all this green around them.'

His Grandad nodded. But the more Kenneth thought about it, the less certain he felt that Mincer wouldn't follow them.

'I'm just going for a walk,' he said at last, uneasy and restless. 'There's something I want to do.'

Grandad Rogers watched him walk away, then settled down on the grass, tipping his hat over his face. Forty winks would be just nice.

Kenneth looked round the area where they were going to stay the night. One thing was sure, he wasn't going to be caught out again.

There were long stretches of grass, broken by small hillocks and deep natural hollows. There were straggles of trees and then sudden deep coppices of oak and ash, birch and holly. There were treacherous marshy patches and hawthorn hedges dense with head-high cow parsley.

The whole of the area was criss-crossed with dusty stony lanes and secret pathways no wider than Kenneth's foot.

Everywhere there seemed to be the glint of the river, as it snaked through and round the golden smiling country.

Kenneth soon found exactly what he was looking for. Then, he searched until his eye caught the dull gleam of an old square oil can. He pulled the can free from its bed of nettles and laid it on the ground.

Clunk, clunk, clunk! He jumped on the smooth tin until it was nicely flattened. After a lot of thought, he started work and when he'd finished, the sun was low in the sky and he was almost as hot and dirty as he'd been when they had first stopped.

He wandered back to the river, woke his Grandad, had another quick wash, and then Grandad showed him how to cut willow wands, two or three from each clump so that it looked as if no-one had been there.

'Now we can weave them together,' his Grandad said.

Kenneth worked hard. The willow was tough on his fingers and the sap marked his skin. They gathered the huge dock leaves and thin whippy grasses, threading them in and out of the willow. In the end, they had two long, narrow, green igloos.

'These will give us good shelter,' the old man said, satisfied. 'I shouldn't think it'll rain. We look as if we're in for a fine night.'

'Yes,' Kenneth agreed but, inwardly, he thought it might not be such a fine night after all.

Not at all.

Chapter Four

WHILST KENNETH AND Grandad Rogers had been working, the boy had heard continual long low whistles, which chuckled and trilled like a wild bird's song.

Several times he had stopped work and glanced around but there had been nothing to see.

After a while, Grandad grew tired.

'I think I'll turn in now,' he said in a weary voice, and slowly he tucked himself into his green shelter.

Kenneth sat on; then, hearing a scuffling in the clump of bushes that flanked the field, he walked towards them, fists clenched.

There was nothing there. Kenneth

pushed his way through the hedge over to the far side. Still nothing.

He looked up at the sky. A thin sickle moon was riding high. 'Whooooooo!' the long wailing sound came almost from his elbow. 'Whooooooo!' it went again and, out of the raggy bushes and blackberry strands, there rose the grinning face of Mincer Muggs.

'Did I scare you, cloth head?' Mincer asked roughly.

'You don't scare me,' Kenneth retorted, wishing his heart wouldn't jump so.

'Oh, I see,' Mincer sneered. 'I don't scare the tramp. Well, try this for size.' He lifted his hands. Around him emerged the hard mean faces of every member of his gang.

Kenneth swallowed.

'We're gonna teach you a lesson, Grey,' Mincer went on, then slowly started to push his way towards the boy. 'You – and that smelly old man you call Grandad.'

Kenneth stared at them. He felt winded by their appearance.

'Don't you touch my Grandad.'

Mincer waved the walloping stick at him.

'You gonna stop me?' he crowed. 'Same as you did last time?' and he and the boys with him sniggered.

The Muggs gang all had sticks in their hands. Heavy pieces of wood. Some still with the leaves on them.

Kenneth took a step back, then another and another. There was a bleak terrible moment, then, 'Get him!' Mincer roared, and Kenneth turned and fled.

He flew up the side of the field as if he had wings on his heels. He could almost feel Mincer's hot sour breath on the back of his neck. Desperately, he pushed himself on. In front lay a thick spread of leaves, hawthorn, thistles, stinging nettles, bright flowers, all growing together.

Kenneth bunched his body tightly and with a tremendous leap, had cleared the dense undergrowth, landing safely on the other side. He stopped, looking back at Mincer.

One by one the Muggs gang tore into the thick clump, hurriedly backing out again with frenzied yelps as the stinging nettles bit into them. The thistles scratched them. The trailing brambles ripped at their hair and brought blood welling up on their skin.

'What do you think you're doing?' Mincer shouted as his gang tottered away from the thick greenery. 'Come back here and get over that . . . that lot,' he finished.

'You get over it,' his gang told him. 'If you want him, you get him because we're not going through there again. Just look at us.'

Mincer sneered they were miserable cowards. His gang didn't take this in good part and, muttering and grumbling, huddled together in a surly group.

'You can all jump over it,' Mincer ordered. 'He did.' But not one of his gang would make a move. 'Then I'll jump first,' Mincer said at last. 'And you lot can follow.'

Kenneth watched them from behind the safety of a fat bush.

Mincer moved back so that he could get a long run. He bullied his gang into lining up behind him. 'And when I've

gone,' he threatened, 'you lot had better be behind me. Don't forget,' – he lifted the walloping stick – 'I've still got this and I'll use it on anybody who doesn't jump.' He stared blackly at each member of the Muggs gang. 'OK?'

Sullenly, the boys nodded OK.

Mincer took a deep breath as he eyed the wilderness that lay sprawled in front of him. He had a sudden feeling it was like a sleeping lion. He had better not fail.

Holding the walloping stick well clear, he started the run. Faster and faster he went, gathering speed with every step until, with a wild kicking of his legs, he was soaring through the air.

'Made it,' he shouted exultantly when he landed. 'I made it.' Then he turned. 'Now, you lot come. Come on – start running.' He swung back round and caught a glimpse of Kenneth's hair.

He grinned, showing teeth no amount of willow or wild mint would ever clean.

'I'm coming to get you, Grey!' he bellowed.

The thin moon seemed to jump in the sky as if Mincer's voice had disturbed it.

Mincer took a step forward. His gang waited in the still air, clouds of gnats buzzing round them, biting and tormenting them.

'Well, move then,' Mincer flung over his shoulder. 'Move!' And as the first lad almost made a move, he took another step. There was a horrible rending, crashing noise and Mincer Muggs and the walloping stick vanished in front of his gang's terrified eyes.

'He's gone!' they wailed. 'Fallen into the middle of the earth.'

They waited no longer but took to their heels and left their leader to look out for himself.

Chapter Five

KENNETH MOVED OUT of the shelter of the thickly leafed bush and walked over to where Mincer had disappeared. He stared into the pit.

'It was you 'oo done this,' Mincer raged, as he saw Kenneth's face above him. 'I'll skin you alive for this, Grey,' he blustered. 'I'll . . . I'll . . .'

'You'll what?' Kenneth asked. 'You won't do anything because you can't get out of there.'

Mincer glared up at the boy.

'You see if I can't,' he said, and started scrambling up the sides of the pit that had taken Kenneth such a long time to dig with the flattened oil can.

When he had finished deepening the

ditch which lay in front of the tangled greenery, Kenneth had placed long branches over the gaping hole. No-one could have seen it.

At the same time, knowing Muggs all too well, Kenneth had made a besom out of a long scratchy stick, tying fat bunches of juicy green nettles around one end with the wiry whispering grass that sighed and shushed around them. He'd had to be careful there!

The more Mincer tried to climb, the more the sides of the pit crumbled in on him. To make sure Muggs stayed where he was, Kenneth jabbed the green besom at the bully and the full thick nettles scored harsh blows upon Mincer's hands and face. Mincer yelped in pain.

'I should be careful if I were you,' Kenneth warned. 'You're only going to make things worse.'

Mincer stood still, sucking at the red skin and painful white spots on his hands the stinging nettles had left behind. His shoes were full of dirt. His eyes, his hair, his nose, his ears. He was fed up. He wished he'd never left the town. Worse, he was beginning to feel just a little bit scared.

'I'll help you out in the morning,' Kenneth went on, 'if you give me the walloping stick back.'

Mincer raved and bellowed, shouted and roared, but Kenneth was not to be bullied any more.

'The walloping stick,' he said again. 'Or else you stay there – for ever,' he added, hoping Mincer Muggs would get as big a fright as he'd got in the dustbin.

Mincer refused to be parted from the walloping stick.

Kenneth hadn't thought this would happen and didn't really know what to do next.

'Then I'll leave you,' he threatened

finally. 'I'll leave you here all alone.'

Looking up at the sky, both boys could see the high thin moon was very bright and clear. But there were clouds milling up and darkness was falling fast.

'That moon won't look so bright behind a cloud,' Kenneth said. 'And it can be very dark at the bottom of a hole. Give me the walloping stick and . . . and I'll give you a light.'

Mincer looked at the black walls of the pit. He was scared.

'All right, then,' he snarled. 'Give me the light first, though.'

Kenneth sped silently back to camp, frightened Muggs would manage to climb out whilst he was gone. He rummaged in Grandad's rucksack and found the torch. He switched it on and off: the beam of light was as clear as day. How much he hoped all this would teach Mincer the lesson Grandad said he needed.

He was cautious going back. Nearing the hole, he lay flat on his stomach and wriggled across the open grass. If

Muggs was out, he for one didn't want to get caught. He felt cold just thinking about that.

When, in the light of the torch, Kenneth saw Mincer huddled at the bottom of the pit, he heaved a sigh of relief.

'Here,' he growled. 'Pass up the walloping stick and I'll give you the light.'

After a brief silence, Mincer handed up the stick and Kenneth passed down the torch.

'You can't leave me down 'ere all night,' Mincer wailed but Kenneth said grimly that he could and would.

He dragged up the green igloo and set it down beside the hole. Then, he slid under it and watched the sky. He wanted to scare Muggs but he didn't want anything bad to happen to him.

All night he kept guard although there was no sound from the pit. By the first light of dawn, Kenneth finally fell asleep and it was then that Mincer Muggs, heart thumping like an old tin drum, managed to make his escape.

The gang leader stood in the cool quiet land, staring round with eyes so fierce they almost burnt the grass.

He didn't see Kenneth. The green igloo melted into the green around it. It wasn't until Mincer moved forward and stepped on Kenneth that he knew he was there.

Kenneth woke up with a frightening suddenness. As soon as he saw what had happened, he rolled over and over in the igloo, rolling and tumbling out of the way of Mincer's big feet.

No matter how fast he moved, he couldn't escape. Mincer bent down and

tore the shelter off him, dragging him up by the scruff of his neck and nearly choking Kenneth by twisting the neck of his jumper.

'Urg. Urg,' Kenneth croaked and Mincer shook the boy.

''Oo's going to do what now?' he asked meanly.

Kenneth could just see the walloping stick. He realised he still had a chance but he had to act fast.

With a sudden wrenching twist and wriggle, he tore free and dropped to his knees. In one smooth movement, he had scooped the walloping stick into his fists.

Mincer stepped back, his eyes on the stick and on the boy. Without taking his stare off them, he bent down and seized up a thick knot of wood.

'Now look 'ere, Grey,' he warned.

'One of us is going to walk away and it ain't going to be you.'

Mincer lashed out at Kenneth and Kenneth fended him off with the walloping stick. On and on the struggle went. First Mincer seemed to be winning, then Kenneth gained ground.

Mincer struck one blow that tore the skin off Kenneth's knuckles. Kenneth fought back with the walloping stick.

He felt tired, worn out. It was almost as if they were fighting in the old old way, with lances instead of sticks. Then, through the woods behind them, came a long echoing roar.

'MINCERRRRRRRRR!' The huge voice filled the sky.

'MINCERRRRRRR,' it went again and the dawn birds chattered with fear.

'WHERE ARRRRRRRRRE YOU?'

Mincer went pale. He stood in front

of Kenneth, stick in hand, and gulped.

'Cor blimey,' he groaned. 'That's my Dad. Wait till I get my mitts on that gang of mine. They've gone and snitched on me, they 'ave. I'll kill 'em. I'll –'

'M I N C E RRRRRR!'

Mincer trembled.

''Ere,' he said suddenly. 'Give us a hand. Don't let 'im see me,' he pleaded. 'He'll skin me alive getting him out 'ere. Where's that green thing?' He looked round frantically. 'Let me hide under that, will yer?'

Without thinking, Kenneth looked for the green igloo and then dragged it over to Mincer. The bully lay down and pulled it over his body, tucking his head out of the way.

''ERE!' A great roar came over to Kenneth. 'You seen that lad of mine?'

Kenneth shook his head dumbly.

The huge man staring at him grumbled, 'Wait till I get my hands on him. Is he for the high jump! 'E'll cop it, stopping out all night. Just wait till I see 'im, that's all. He's going to get a taste of this.' He cracked the heavy belt he was carrying against a tree trunk.

Kenneth shivered.

'You sure you ain't seen him?' Mr Muggs asked suspiciously but Kenneth shook his head again.

'I haven't see him. Not at all.'

Mincer's Dad hesitated, running the belt again and again through his fingers. Then, with heavy decision, he fastened it back on and stumbled away through the woods.

Kenneth had to take a deep breath. His legs were shaking. 'Poor old Mincer,' he thought suddenly, surprised by the thought.

He stared down at the green igloo.

'It's all right,' he said. 'You can come out now. He's gone.' And the gang leader crawled out, white faced.

Mincer stood up.

'Er, fanks,' he mumbled, then, slyness returning, wondered if he could possibly jump Grey and get the stick back.

Kenneth watched him, noticing the narrowing of Mincer's eyes. All at once, he didn't feel at all sorry for Mincer Muggs. He clutched the walloping stick more tightly than ever.

'Go on, Mincer,' he ordered sharply.

'You get off home else I'll shout your Dad back.'

Mincer kicked the grass and then, grumbling, turned unwillingly back towards the town.

Kenneth watched him shamble away. He didn't lay the stick down and start to fill in the pit until he was certain Mincer had really gone.

By the time he'd finished and made his way back to camp, his Grandad had woken up.

'Now then, Kenneth,' he said cheerfully. 'Time for breakfast and then . . . another lovely day.'

'Another lovely day,' Kenneth echoed and, grinning, handed the walloping stick back to his Grandad.

He was certain of one thing. It would be a long time before Mincer Muggs forgot his night in the country.

Kenneth laughed and then he and Grandad collected twigs.

It was time for breakfast.